MONSTER NEEDS YOUR VOTE

A MONSTER & Me™ BOOK

MONSTER
NEEDS
YOUR VOTE

Story by **PAUL CZAJAK**   *Illustrations by* **WENDY GRIEB**

mighty media KIDS

MINNEAPOLIS, MINNESOTA

Text copyright © 2015 Paul Czajak
Illustrations copyright © 2015 Wendy Grieb

Published by Mighty Media Kids, an imprint of Mighty Media Press,
a division of Mighty Media, Inc.

LIBRARY OF CONGRESS CATALOGING-IN-PUBLICATION DATA
Czajak, Paul.
 Monster needs your vote / story by Paul Czajak ; illustrations by
Wendy Grieb. -- First edition.
     pages cm. -- (A Monster & me book)
 ISBN 978-1-938063-63-3 (hardback) -- ISBN 978-1-938063-64-0
(ebook)
[1. Stories in rhyme. 2. Elections--Fiction. 3. Politics, Practical--
Fiction. 4. Monsters--Fiction.] I. Grieb, Wendy, illustrator. II. Title.
 PZ8.3.C9975Mr 2015
 [E]--dc23
                     2015011415

Art Direction and book design by Anders Hanson, Mighty Media, Inc.

Printed and manufactured in the United States
North Mankato, Minnesota

Distributed by Publishers Group West

First edition

10 9 8 7 6 5 4 3 2 1

PAUL CZAJAK got an F with
the words "get a tutor" on his college
writing paper and, after that, never
thought he'd become a writer. But
after spending 20 years as a chemist,
he knew his creativity could no longer
be contained. He lives in New Jersey
with his wife and two little monsters.
In addition to the Monster & Me™
series, he's also the author of *Seaver
the Weaver*.

WENDY GRIEB is a professional
working in the Los Angeles animation
industry and teaching animation.
She is also an Annie Award–winning
storyboard artist, who has worked as
a developmental artist, illustrator,
and character designer for companies
such as Disney, Nickelodeon, Sony,
Klasky-Csupo, White Wolf, and more.
She lives in Yorba Linda, California.

Dedication

To all the LIBRARIANS in the world.

Your passion keeps our books alive!

Monster needs
to cast his vote
to pick the president.

"I want to be
a part of this
incredible event!"

I said to Monster, "Don't be mad.
I know it may
sound mean.

But you are not
allowed to vote.
You need to be eighteen."

"Then I will run for president,"
Monster said to me.

"I'll give a voice to young and old,
from two to ninety-three."

"Monster, what's your platform?
Why should people vote for you?"

"Summer should be longer and a fix is overdue."

He grabbed a soapbox,
went to town, and talked about
the seasons.

How summer should be twice as long ...
and listed *several* reasons.

Monster's
oratory skills were
filled with monster flair.

But no one stopped to listen,
and the people left the square.

"Monster, maybe summer isn't what the voters need.
Perhaps a change of issues if you're going to succeed?"

"Dessert for dinner," Monster said,
"is where my passion lies."

So Monster ran on eating sweets,
which seemed a bit unwise.

"A chocolate cake on every plate, a pie in every pot."

Monster spoke
at Town Hall,
but his words
were all
for naught.

I said to Monster, "I don't think they're interested in treats. You'll need a different issue to get voters in these seats."

"I'm confused with politics and what it's all about.

No one seems to like me, so I guess I'll just drop out."

Monster looked discouraged. He was ready to resign.

But he became inspired
when he saw a CLOSING sign.

PUBLIC LIBRARY
CLOSING

"The library is closing.
That's a crime that can't take place!
To fail on education is a national disgrace!"

We started with a grassroots movement, going door to door. With posters saying, "Reading Turns Your Voice into a ROAR!"

Protecting schools and learning tools was Monster's major mission.

And in debates, from state to state, he crushed the opposition.

The voters loved his message, and his campaign came alive!

That is, until they realized that he wasn't thirty-five.

"Monster, you're not old enough to be the president.

The law's the law. We have to stop. There is no argument."

You must be 35 years old to run for president of the United States

"It's not about me winning but the message I convey.

A fight for education, I hope, never goes away."

Monster was persistent, and his message kept on growing.

Even on Election Day ...

there were no signs of slowing.

Monster made
a difference,
though he was
too young to run.

And Monster's roar in politics had only just begun!